The drawings in Zebedee's Balloon
are two-tone illustrations,
using the technique of wood engraving.

© Éditions Auzou, Paris (France), 2011
(English version)
ISBN: 978-2-7338-1942-5
General Manager: Gauthier Auzou
Senior Editor: Florence Pierron
English Version Editor: Nelson Yomtov
Graphics and layout: Annaïs Tassone
Original Title: *Le ballon de Zébulon*
Translation: Susan Allen Maurin

Printed and bound in China, 2011.

Zebedee's Balloon

Text by Alice Brière-Haquet
Illustrations by Olivier Philipponneau

AUZOU

Zebedee has a lovely red balloon,
which he calls "Ball",
That is just as soft as cotton wool.
Ball is like a cuddly toy
And it gives Zebedee a lot of joy.
Ball is his friend who is always there,
And it goes with Zebedee everywhere.

But sadly, one evening, Ball disappears,
And Zebedee is alone in the dark and in tears.

Lost in the night without Ball,
Zebedee feels very, very small.
Suddenly... he hears a noise in the night
That comes from behind him and gives him a fright!

It is the old owl perched in a tree
That is looking out, as always, eagerly.

The owl tries to soothe his fears,
"Little Zebedee, please dry your tears.
Together, as we search hard for Ball,
You will make not one but ten friends in all!"

The friends search in the night together,
When suddenly they see it... yes, over there!

Just in front of them, not far at all,
Right in the middle... isn't it Ball?

But, no, it is a thicket of pretty red flowers
Where two lovely doves have been cooing for hours.

Zebedee is sad, as you can imagine,
But his friends do their best to comfort him.

The doves try to soothe his fears,
"Little Zebedee, please dry your tears.
Together, as we search hard for Ball,
You will make not one but ten friends in all!"

The friends search in the night together,
When suddenly, they see it... yes, over there!

Look, it is not far from us at all.
Just down there, careful, do not fall!

But it is only wild strawberries in a bunch
And three hungry snails having a munch.

Zebedee is upset, as you can imagine
But his friends do their best to comfort him.

The snails try to soothe his fears,
"Little Zebedee, please dry your tears.
Together, as we search hard for Ball,
You will make not one but ten friends in all!"

The friends search in the night together,
When suddenly, they see it... yes, over there!

Hey! Ho! Look up to the sky!
There it is, way up high...!

But it is only an apple tree that they can see
And Zebedee angrily kicks the tree.

An apple falls and hits him on the nose.
There are four worms inside having a doze.

The worms try to soothe his fears,
"Little Zebedee, please dry your tears.
Together, as we search hard for Ball,
You will make not one but ten friends in all!"

1

2

3

4

And off they go, once again,
Zebedee and all his new friends...

Wait!... Let us count from one to ten:

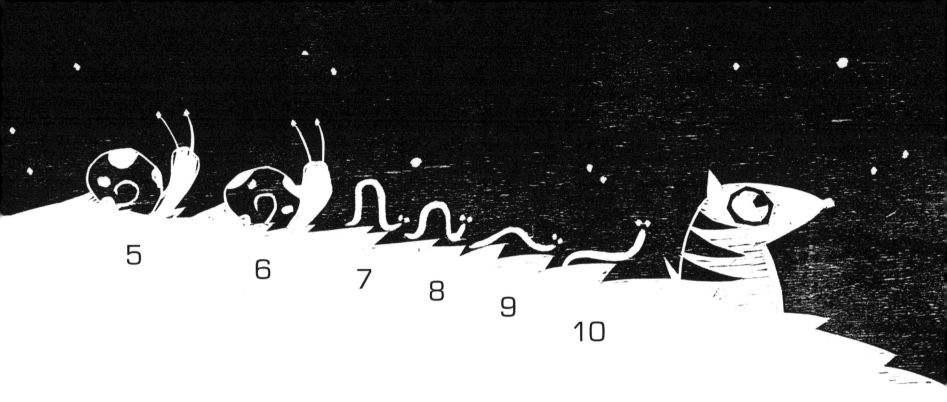

5
6
7
8
9
10

1 owl, 2 doves, 3 snails, 4 worms = 10 friends

One friend is lost, but ten friends have been found...
And that is a very fine amount!

Dear little Ball, wherever you may be,
You can live your own life, because, you see,
You need not worry, everything is alright,
Zebedee is no longer afraid of the night.